The

Happy

Draydel

by RUTH SAMUELS

Illustrated By EZEKIEL SCHLOSS

KTAV PUBLISHING HOUSE, INC.

In the middle of the town was a toy shop with
every kind of toy you could imagine—
Toys for boys and toys for girls.
Beautiful dolls with golden curls.

Toy automobiles and electric trains,
Fire engines and trucks and shining jet planes.
There was even a draydel that had been de-
livered to the store by mistake.

But, what a handsome draydel it was! It was
made of metal, bright as gold, and on each
side of it was painted a Hebrew letter; a
NUN, a GIMMEL, a HAY and a SHEEN.
And what did these four letters mean?

They meant "NESS GADOL HAYAW SHOM," "a great miracle happened there." And when you play the draydel game, the NUN stands for "take nothing," the GIMMEL for "take everything," the HAY for "take half" and the SHEEN for "take all."

Now, wouldn't you think that such a wonderful draydel would be the happiest toy in all the world? But alas, the little Hebrew top was lonely and sad. For each night at midnight, when all the toys came to life, it lay alone and forgotten upon the shelf.

The toy soldiers marched and the fire engines clanged their bells and the jet planes zoomed overhead together like a flock of birds.

But the sad little draydel didn't have even one other top to spin with.

One winter day a woman came into the shop
with her little boy.
"He wants to choose a Chanukah gift for
himself," she told the owner.
The boy looked around at all the toys. Then
suddenly he cried out:

"Oh look! There's a draydel! That's what I want for Chanukah!"

And so the little boy took the draydel home. "At last!" thought the happy little top, "I have found somebody who will play with me!"

The next day was the first day of Chanukah. Everyone in the house was busy as a bee. The little draydel watched in wonder as the boy ran from room to room, hanging up colored decorations.

The father polished the menorah until it shone like the sun.

From the spic-and-span kitchen came a delightful aroma — for mother was cooking delicious latkes.

But in all this excitement nobody was pay-
ing any attention to the little draydel. It
lay all by itself on a window sill, lonelier
than ever.
Then the draydel saw the family gather
around the menorah. Father lighted a little

candle and with it lighted the other candle
in the menorah and said a blessing. Then the
whole family sang Mo-oz Tzur.

"Good Yom Tov — Happy Chanukah!"
said the father when the song was over.

"Happy Chanukah!" everybody answered.

"Now I play with my draydel!" laughed
the boy.

Running to the window sill, he picked up the draydel and took it to his father.

"Father," he asked, "do you remember what the four letters on the draydel mean?"
"Long, long ago in Palestine," said father, "the land that belonged to the Children of Israel was conquered by the Syrians.

"These wicked men captured the city of Jerusalem and the holy temple of God. But the great Jewish hero, Judah Maccabbee, gathered together an army. After many long years of battle, Judah and his brave men drove the Syrians from Jerusalem.

"But the beautiful temple had become broken and dirty. The light no longer burned in the holy Menorah. Judah and his men cleaned and polished until the temple was like new again. They cleaned the great Menorah, too. Then the high priest poured into it holy oil from the last flask.

"'Alas,' he said, 'there is just enough oil to

burn for one day.'

"But then — Ness Gadol Hayaw Shom! A great miracle happened! The light in the Menorah burned for eight days and eight nights! That is why there are eight candles in the menorah. And that is why Jews all over the world celebrate Chanukah at this time every year."

Had the draydel heard right? It made his
head spin! And suddenly, from the tip of its
top to the top of its stem, it was filled with
pride and joy.

Then the little boy gave the stem a twist.
Round and round the little top went spin-
ning, flashing like a little golden sun, before

the lighted candle in the menorah.
"A great miracle happened there," hummed
the draydel to itself. "That's what my letters mean! What a wonderful thing it is to
be a draydel! I'd rather be a draydel than any
toy in all the world!"